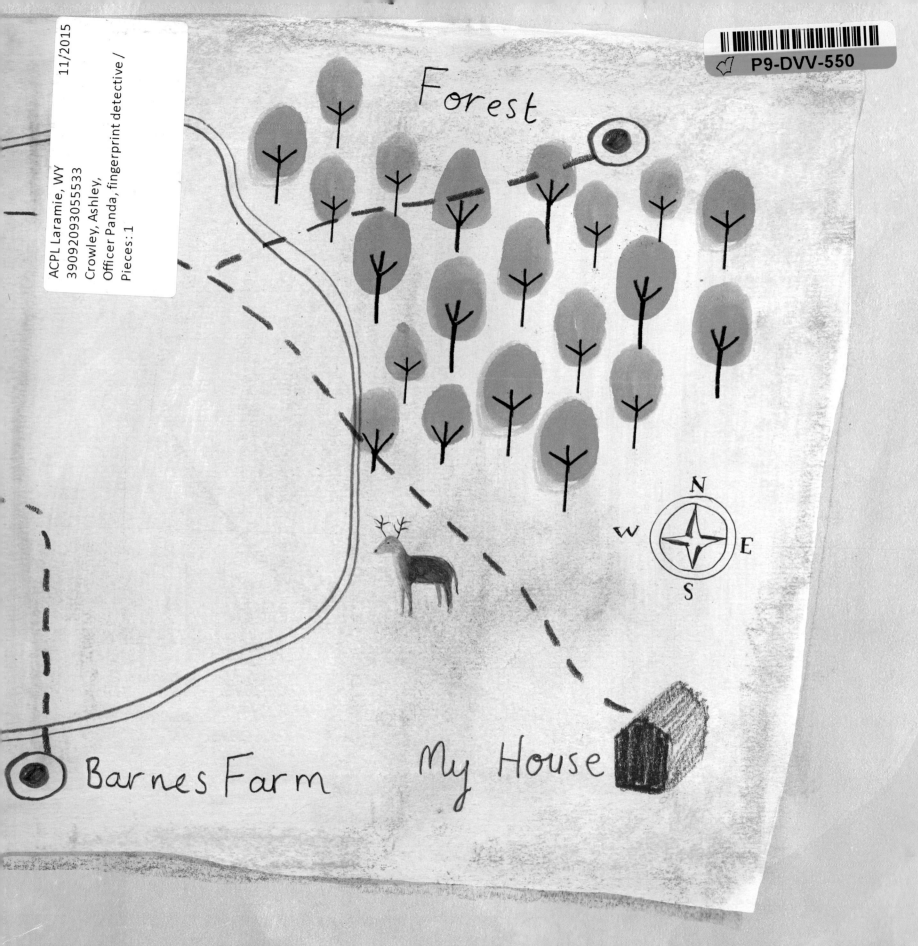

Forest

My House

Barnes Farm

N
W   E
S

for my boy,
FRANKIE
x

THANKYOU

ISBN 978-0-06-236626-9

The artist used mixed media, including pencils, colored pencils, inks, gouache paint, and graphite sticks,
and Adobe Photoshop to create the illustrations for this book. Typography by Martha Rago
15 16 17 18 19 SCP 10 9 8 7 6 5 4 3 2 1
❖
First Edition

Officer Panda

Fingerprint Detective

BY

ASHLEY CROWLEY

HARPER
An Imprint of HarperCollinsPublishers

5:15 P.M.: OFFICER PANDA MAKES SOME NOTES BEFORE HEADING HOME.

HE LOOKED CLOSER . . .

AND CLOSER . . .

IT'S YOU!

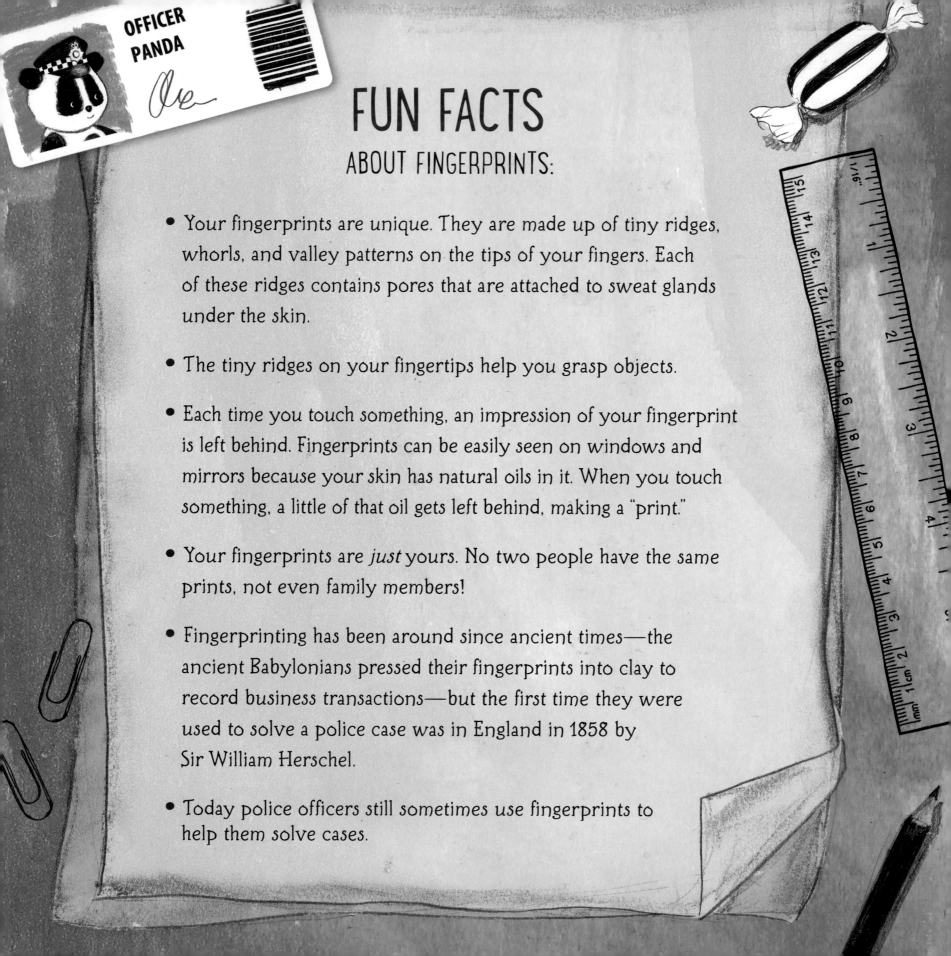

FUN FACTS
ABOUT FINGERPRINTS:

- Your fingerprints are unique. They are made up of tiny ridges, whorls, and valley patterns on the tips of your fingers. Each of these ridges contains pores that are attached to sweat glands under the skin.

- The tiny ridges on your fingertips help you grasp objects.

- Each time you touch something, an impression of your fingerprint is left behind. Fingerprints can be easily seen on windows and mirrors because your skin has natural oils in it. When you touch something, a little of that oil gets left behind, making a "print."

- Your fingerprints are *just* yours. No two people have the same prints, not even family members!

- Fingerprinting has been around since ancient times—the ancient Babylonians pressed their fingerprints into clay to record business transactions—but the first time they were used to solve a police case was in England in 1858 by Sir William Herschel.

- Today police officers still sometimes use fingerprints to help them solve cases.

OFFICER PANDA